Charlie the Horse

By Deanie Humphrys-Dunne

Illustrated by Holly Humphrys-Bajaj

PublishAmerica
Baltimore

First printing

PublishAmerica has allowed this work to remain exactly as the author intended, verbatim, without editorial input.

ISBN: 978-1-4489-8672-9
PUBLISHED BY PUBLISHAMERICA, LLLP
www.publishamerica.com
Baltimore

Printed in the United States of America

Dedication

This book is dedicated to Francis, Holly and Prem, whose encouragement and inspiration made this story possible

Ben'sHailey

Enjoy Charlee's adven-
tures,

Dearee Humphrus-
Dunne

Charlie the Horse

The Debut

"Hello Charlie," the baby horse's mom said. "You are so handsome! You have my black hair and a crooked white blaze on your face like your daddy has. You have four white stockings like your daddy, too. Just look at those long legs. I'll bet you will be a famous racehorse like your dad, Charles the Great. I am going to name you Charlie the Horse. How do you like it in this big world here in Kentucky? We can talk like people, but we only talk with the other animals here at Racing Haven Farm. I'll bet you are hungry, Charlie. You need to drink a lot of milk so you grow big and strong. Race horses need to work hard so they need strong bones and muscles." *Charlie thought there are so many things to explore in the world. I wonder what the life of a famous racehorse would be like.*

Charlie's coat, or the hair covering his body, was soft and thick. "Do you know why your hair is so thick Charlie? It's nature's way of protecting you so that you won't get hurt if you scrape against something."

"That's a good thing, Mama," Charlie said. "I bump into things sometimes. It seems like I have so many legs. One goes this way and one goes that way. I'm just not sure where I'll end up."

"Don't worry, dear. You have to get used to things in this world. You'll figure it all out. Today we are going out to the field so you can taste the yummy green grass in the pasture. You will love it. Soon you will meet some of the other foals (baby horses) here at the farm. They will all try to become famous racehorses just like you. However, they don't know that you have many famous racehorses in your family. You're going to have a lot of talent that some of the others won't have," said Mama. *I hope I make lots of friends here and we can play together Charlie thought.*

Charlie munched the lush green grass. He stayed close to his mom and she watched over him closely. "This is your playground, Charlie. You can run and

Baby Charlie the Horse and his Mama

play here. I'll watch over you and you can start running a little while you're here," said his Mom. "You can trot around the field (slow jog). You can even canter here (slow gallop) because there are no stones anywhere or holes in the ground that could hurt you." Charlie watched his mom before going back to munching the grass. *I love the taste of dandelions and tulips. Yum! They are a nice dessert.* "It's nice being in the world, Mama," he said. "It's pretty here. I can't wait to meet some of the other baby horses. I hope I can run faster than any of the others."

"I'll bet you will, Charlie. I have a feeling you're going to run very fast and it will be fun for you," said Mama. "We will spend time together and I will help you by telling you about the life of a racehorse. I'll take you around the barn and introduce you to some of the other horses. The most famous one is General Quick. He's a retired racehorse. He's famous for winning some of the biggest races like the Kentucky Derby. People still come from far away to visit him. When you are older, he can advise you so you'll know what to expect when you start your training. You'll recognize him. He's the big, freckled gray horse. He's friendly. All the young horses go to him for advice."

"Oh, I can't wait to talk to him, Mama. I'll learn lots about what racehorses do. Right now, I like to run and play in the field with you watching over me. I want to be the best race horse around when I grow up." *I wonder how hard it is to be a famous racehorse. Do I have what it takes?*

"Look how much you've grown already," said Charlie's Mom. "You've lost your baby hair and you are getting so tall. You'll be a year old before long. I can't wait to see how handsome you are then."

A few days later Charlie's mom took him around the barn to meet some of the other foals and General Quick. The little foals had their own barn. "Hello Charlie," they said. "We've heard about you already. We want to play together. We want to know which one of us is the fastest."

"Oh, I can't wait!" said Charlie. "It's a date." *I wonder how fast I'll be. Will I be as good a racehorse as my dad was? Will I be clumsy? Will I be better than the other baby horses?*

Playing Tag

Finally, Charlie got his chance to play in the field with Glory and Buddy, two colts his age. Glory was tall and brown and Buddy was reddish with a white blaze down his face.

"Hey, fellas can we play tag to see who can run the fastest? We don't have to touch each other, just see who's the fastest. I think I'm the tallest, but that doesn't mean I'm the fastest," said Charlie.

"Good idea," Glory and Buddy hollered.

"We'll race three times around the pasture," said Charlie. "Okay, Ready, set, go!" Glory quickly cantered to the lead, with Buddy close behind and Charlie at the end of the line. On the second lap, Charlie flew past Buddy and in the blink of an eye. He was along side of Glory, fighting for the lead. He just managed to put his neck in front of Glory by the end of the last lap. *Whew! I made it. I was the fastest. I don't want to hurt Glory and Buddy's feelings, though. I want them to feel good about trying their hardest to win.*

Buddy, Charlie and Glory playing tag

"Gee, Charlie you surely are fast," said Glory. "I thought I'd beat you but you passed me at the last minute."

"Don't worry, Glory. I was surprised too. I think I'm going to like running. Still, I don't know much about it. I'll have a chat with General Quick later today and find out some more stuff about this runnin' business. Now that I'm older, my room is right across from his so we can talk whenever we want," Charlie said.

Getting to Know
the General

"Hey, General," said Charlie. "Tell me about racing. What's it like?"

"It's tricky, but it's a lot of fun. The idea is you have to try to run faster than any of the other horses do. At first, you'll go in easy races, but they will get harder when you have experience in more races," said General.

"What if I am tired and I don't want to race?" asked Charlie.

"Well, you still have to try your best. Sometimes when you get going, you get in a better mood because you really like to run," said General.

"Okay, I'll try to remember that. Will I be able to stay here while I'm learning?"

"No, Charlie, you will need to go to a special barn for training," said General.

"I don't think I want to go," Charlie said, stamping his foot. "I like it here. I'll miss Glory and Buddy. It just wouldn't be the same." *I'll miss my mama too, but I'm supposed to be growing up so I won't say that.*

"That's true, but training is part of growing up. Besides, if you are dreaming of winning the big races like the Kentucky Derby, you have to work hard. You have to run so your muscles will be strong. You have to build your endurance so you won't be tired because some of the races are long. Remember you have a nice owner and they will have the best trainers.

Maybe your trainer will be Misty Canby. She's kind. She will always see that you have everything you need."

"Well, I'll try to remember that, but I will be sad without you, Mom, and all my friends here," said Charlie.

"We will all hear the news about what you are doing. We will be proud of you because we will know you are doing what you are meant to do.

You will become a star if you remember how important it is not to give up when you have a bad day. We all have them, but we must overcome our fears. You need to stay focused on what you want most and you will do fine," said General.

"I'll try my best. We will need to talk more before I leave for training so you can teach me as much as you can. Maybe I should give you a professor's hat. I saw one. They are a funny shape and they have gold strings hanging from one side," Charlie said.

"Oh, you are thinking of the hats called mortar boards. People wear them at graduations. Sometimes teachers wear them, too."

"What a funny name for a hat. Who would want to wear a board on their head?" said Charlie.

"It is a funny name, but that's what it's called. It isn't really a board on your head," said General.

Time just flew by for Charlie. He loved racing in the field with his friends, but he knew that he was nearly old enough to leave for the training farm. The day finally arrived. He stopped to chat with Glory and Buddy.

"Well, guys, this is it. I'm off to the working world now. I'll be looking for you at the races. Remember to do your best when it's your turn for training and racing," Charlie told them.

"We'll give it our best shot," they told him. "We'll see you around," they said turning away so he wouldn't see the little tears trickling down their faces.

Finally, Charlie stopped by General's stall. "Hey, General do you have any last minute advice for me before I leave? Today's the day. As soon as my legs are bandaged for the trip, I'll be on my way."

"Just concentrate on doing your best. Try to remember when you're racing, don't get stuck where you have no room to run. Sometimes the other horses block you in so it's easier for them to win."

"Okay, I'll try to remember that. Thanks for everything. I'll be thinking of you," Charlie said.

In the Working World

Charlie going to training

Charlie looked out the window of the trailer as it bounced along down the driveway and on to the highway. He took one last look at Racing Haven and tried to think about the new adventures ahead. *I feel sad already, but I have to pretend to be grown up enough to start learning. I have to try my best, even when I miss my mom and my friends.*

It wasn't a very long ride to Sweetbrier Racing Stable. *There are so many barns and racetracks, but I'm glad there are fields too so I can play.*

Mr. Bains, the barn manager came out to greet Charlie.

"Hello there, big fella," he said, as he patted Charlie on the neck.

"There's a whole new world waiting for you here. You'll be a working man from now on, but Misty Canby will train you. She's the best around." *"Oh boy! I got Misty for my trainer! I really wanted her because the General said she is the best.*

Mr. Bains led Charlie to a big stall. He could look out the window and watch some of the horses training, or relaxing in the fields. Jimmy, one of the farm workers, came by Charlie's stall. "Hi Charlie. You and I are going to be good friends. I'll make sure you are comfortable and happy," Jimmy said. "We'll let you settle in for a couple of days before you go to work."

Everyone here seems nice, thought Charlie. The working world might not be so bad after all.

The Real Work Starts

Misty stopped by to visit Charlie. "Hi, big guy. We're going to be best friends. We are starting your training today. There is nothing to fear. You need to learn many new things before you start racing. I think it's like kids going to school. They do the easy things first."

Good, Charlie thought. It's going to be the easy stuff first. Nothing too scary here at Sweetbrier Racing Stable.

The first day of training was different than Charlie expected. Misty put sand bags on his back. "This will help you get used to carrying weight. You need to know how it feels before we put a person on you." As if that were not enough, she put a metal thing in his mouth. It was part of a leather thing on his head.

"This is the bridle. When you are racing, the jockey will steer you by using the reins in his hands," she said. Misty walked Charlie around the round pen outside of the barn so he could feel the weight on his back. Charlie shook his whole body to see if the weight on his back would fall off. It didn't. *Maybe the weight is stuck there. I'll have to get used to it. Maybe if I have a person on me, he will be stuck too.* He tried hopping up and down a little. Still, the weight was there. Misty put the weight on him for a couple weeks until Charlie seemed relaxed with it on his back. After that, she added the saddle with the weights tied on it. *This saddle thing is strange. I have something around my tummy to hold it on. It doesn't really pinch, but I can tell it's there. I heard the people calling it a girth. It keeps the saddle from slipping. Now and then, the people make sure the girth is tight enough so the saddle doesn't slide. I can hold my breath and make my tummy a little bigger so people don't make the girth too tight. I can do that little trick if I want. Then when they're not looking, I can breathe again and I have a tiny bit more space between my tummy and the girth.*

Charlie and Misty in the round pen

Carrying a Person Around

Charlie met a young lady named Kerry. She was an exercise girl. Her job was to teach Charlie how to behave with a person on him. She sat gently on him. He didn't seem to be afraid so she urged him to move forward by squeezing the saddle with her legs. He stood still. "Come on, Charlie, walk forward," she said. He took two steps before stopping again. "No, Charlie, keep going," she told him, squeezing the saddle again. *I think I'm getting the idea. I'm supposed to keep going when I feel Kerry's legs.* He kept walking. *I wonder if I should walk all day. How do I know when to stop?* Suddenly, he felt Kerry pull back hard on the reins. "Whoa, Charlie!" Charlie stopped short, almost making Kerry lose her balance. *Okay, I think I've got the idea now. When Kerry squeezes the saddle with her legs, I'm supposed to move forward and when I feel the metal thing against my mouth, I'm supposed to stop.*

Kerry practiced walking around on Charlie and then they progressed to trotting. Charlie did well; however, he was a curious fellow. He liked to stop to look at things along the way. He seemed to notice everything, even the little things like butterflies that fluttered by. *Whenever I see those daffodils and tulips, I'd like to snack on them, even if I'm working. I guess I'm supposed to work a little more and snack a little less now that I'm growing up.*

Before long, Charlie was cantering around with Kerry on him. They were good friends now. Kerry talked to him often. She wanted to explain everything to him so he wouldn't be afraid of anything new. Charlie understood that when Kerry squeezed her leg hard against the saddle and moved her weight more forward he was supposed to canter faster. A fast canter is called a gallop. Kerry galloped him around the training track one day when suddenly Charlie noticed the tulips lining the edge of the ring. He stopped short, nearly causing Kerry to fall.

"Charlie, what are you doing?" she scolded. Then she noticed that Charlie couldn't resist nibbling on the flowers. "You silly boy. You should be working, not munching the flowers!" *I'm a growing boy. Aren't I supposed to keep my strength up?*

Introducing
the Starting Gate

Charlie had been at Sweetbrier Racing Stable for nearly three months when Misty decided it was time to introduce him to the starting gate.

Charlie was calm. He cantered around the training ring. Then he saw it. *What is that strange looking thing? It looks like a bunch of tiny stalls on wheels. I wonder what you do with them.*

"Charlie, these are the starting gates," Kerry explained. Charlie stopped in front of them. He sniffed them. Then he saw Jimmy walk over and lead him inside of one of the stalls. *There isn't much room in here. It's not very comfortable. Hope I don't have to be in here long.* Charlie was fidgeting and wiggling back and forth. *Should I try to back up?* He moved back one-step, but he felt the iron gate behind him. Then Kerry squeezed the saddle with her legs. *I guess I'm supposed to go forward.* He moved one step forward and leaned on the gate. Then he heard a loud bell and the gate sprang open. He stood still, looking around.

Kerry took him back to the starting gate. "The idea is to run when you hear the bell, Charlie," she said. "Let's try again." This time he heard the bell and galloped a few strides, and then he stopped to look around again. Kerry gave him a pat on the neck. "That's better, Charlie. It'll be even better when you learn to keep going. I think that's enough work for today, though," she said. Kerry walked Charlie back to the barn and Jimmy gave him a nice bath. *Hey, this is the good life. I just cantered a few feet and now I get a nice bubble bath.*

Kerry and Misty talked about Charlie's training session. "He did pretty well," said Kerry. "But he doesn't seem to pay attention to his work. He just wants to watch the butterflies and whatever else is around."

"That's true. I couldn't help noticing that too," said Misty. "Next time I think we'll try blinkers and see if that helps," said Misty. "Blinkers are a little hood that fits over the horse's head so that he can only see straight ahead of him. It helps horses to concentrate on their work instead of looking around at everything."

The next day Charlie wore the blinkers for his workout. *These blinker things are strange. I open my eyes wide and I think I should see everything but I can only see things in front of me. What's up with that?*

Kerry jogged him over to the starting gate. This time Charlie walked right in. He pressed his chest against the front, the bell rang and Charlie started running. *Hey, this is fun. I think I like running. I wonder when I'm supposed to stop.* "Good job, Charlie," Kerry said. "Now you're getting the idea. You just run until I tell you to stop." Charlie ran even faster when Kerry leaned forward. She patted his neck and always remembered to tell him he did a good job.

Misty and Kerry talked about Charlie's workout. "He's doing much better with paying attention," Misty said. "He's getting the idea about running. Soon we'll have to see if he can run fast enough to compete in races. I think we should try letting him run with another horse and see how he does. We'll give him a couple days rest and then we'll give it a try."

Charlie relaxed for a couple days, just munching the grass in the field and enjoying the tulips when he wanted dessert. Before long, it was time for working again. Kerry galloped him over to the starting gate. When the bell rang, he noticed something different. He heard hoof beats behind him. *What's going on? Maybe someone wants to play tag with me.* Charlie was still in the lead. Suddenly, the other horse was even with him. They got too close and bumped each other. Charlie didn't know what to do. *Maybe the other horse is mad at me and I should let him go first.* The other horse zoomed by. *I'm a little angry with myself. I let him beat me and I didn't try my best. I remember the General telling me I always have to try my best, even if I'm having a bad day.*

The next day Kerry took Charlie to the racetrack for his workout again. The same horse was in the starting gate next to Charlie. Charlie waited for the bell to ring. He sprang from the gate with long relaxed strides.

He was in the lead for a while before the other horse galloped along side of him. *I'm not going to let you win this time. I'm going to try my best, even if you bump into me.*

Kerry steered Charlie away from the other horse. He kept running faster until the horse was behind him. *Hooray! I like the way it feels to try my best. Besides, it's even better if I win.* "Good job, Charlie. You're really getting the idea now. You're supposed to get to the finish line first so you can be the winner. You get extra oats tonight and a nice bubble bath, too," Kerry said. *Yum! I like the sound of that. Life can't get much better than a big bucket of oats AND a bubble bath on the same day!*

Misty had a talk with the Morton's, Charlie's owners. "I know you have let me make all the decisions about Charlie's training," she said. "He's doing well. In fact, I think he's ready for his first race. He seems to like racing and he learns quickly. If it's alright with you, we'll enter him in the Delmar Race next month."

"That sounds great," said Mr. Morton. "We'll look forward to hearing from you after the race."

Kerry worked Charlie twice a week to get him conditioned for the race. "We don't want to tire you out, big fellow," she said. We just want you in shape for the race." *I'm beginning to really enjoy running. It usually doesn't make me tired, but I don't know what a real race will be like, with horses here, there and everywhere. I wonder how I'll do.*

The First Race

It was finally the day of the race. Charlie woke up early to a big bucket of oats, with some extra vitamins. His coat was so shiny he almost glowed. The sun was shining. Overall, Charlie felt confident. Jimmy even braided his mane (the hair on his neck) so he looked his handsomest. He pranced on to the racetrack. He had a new rider on him because Kerry isn't a jockey. She is an exercise girl. The jockey, Joe Fenton, was well known in the area. He patted Charlie's neck. "Well, Charlie, this is the big day. This is your first race. All you need to do is your best. Everyone around will be proud of you if you do that. When you think about it, that's all anyone can do." Charlie stood quietly in the starting gate. He listened for the bell.

He sprang out of the gate. He was fourth in line early in the race. Joe tried to keep him from being stuck behind any of the horses, but there was nowhere to go. He got stuck behind horses and Joe had to swing to the outside of all of them. Charlie ran as fast as he could, but he was in fourth place when the race was over. *Gee, I tried, but there was nowhere to go so we had to go way to the outside and that gave the other horses a chance to outrun me. I remember the General telling me to try not to get stuck behind horses. I hope Misty and Kerry aren't disappointed.*

Jimmy came to lead him off the racetrack after the race. "Good job, Charlie. You should be proud. You probably would have been in second place if you weren't stuck in traffic. I know you did your best. Don't worry.

There will be plenty of other races." Jimmy gave Charlie a nice walk around to cool him out and then he got a bath and rub down for his legs. *Well, even losing isn't THAT bad. I would be sad, except that I really did try. I still got a bath and rub down. Imagine what will happen when I win.*

Charlie relaxed and played in the fields for a week before his first race. Then Kerry and Misty decided to enter him in the Donley Fair Race in three weeks. "We've got three weeks to train for the next race," Misty said. "Charlie has matured quite a bit. He's much more muscular now and he understands that racing is his job. I think he'll do much better this time. He's had more practice working on the track with other horses. That should help."

I wonder what my next race will be like. Will I get stuck in a wall of horses again? Will I be able to pass everyone and win? Will I be confident?

It was race day again for Charlie. He got a big breakfast just about the time the sun was rising. Jimmy came in to groom him and braid his mane. Charlie stamped his foot and bounced up and down in his stall. "It's Okay, Charlie. You're going to do well today. I just have that feeling," Jimmy said. "Besides you will be the handsomest horse there. All the others will be jealous of how handsome you are and that's before you show them how fast you can run!" *It's nice if I'm handsome, but it's more important that I'm the best racehorse I can be.*

Getting to Know
a New Place

Charlie galloped to the starting gate. Joe was his jockey again. "Okay, Charlie. This is your chance to show them what you can do. The last time was just practice." Charlie could hardly wait for the bell. He flew out of the starting gate this time. Joe was standing straight up in the saddle, pulling the reins so Charlie didn't go too fast too soon. "Steady, boy. I'll let you know when to fly by everybody," he whispered to Charlie. Charlie tried to relax. This time they stayed in the clear. There was no wall of horses to block them. Joe saw an opening by the rail. He quickly positioned Charlie so he could slide through and save ground. There were two horses in front of him. Joe whispered, "Now, Charlie. Go as fast as you can!" Charlie raced by the leaders. *I don't think they knew I was coming! Hooray! I LOVE to surprise them like that!* Charlie heard the crowd roar. Everyone clapped for him. Jimmy walked him into a place called "The Winner's Circle" that is shaped like a horseshoe and it's saved just for the winner of the race. Joe jumped off Charlie's back. "Good job, boy. You showed everyone what you could do today." Charlie got extra oats, a rub down, a bubble bath and some nice compliments for his work that day. *Winning means I get an extra surprise. I get a whole group of pretty flowers put on my neck. They make me look special, but I wish I could eat them.*

A Big Test

Misty called Mr. Morton right after Charlie's first win to tell him the good news. "Charlie won! He did a great job. Joe had him squeeze though the space on the rail and he zoomed by everybody," she said. "I think we should enter him in his first stakes race. It'll be tougher competition for him, but I think he'll love that," Misty said.

Mr. Morton said, "Go for it! I don't mind that stakes races cost money; I can't wait to see what happens. You are doing a fine job with him, Misty. Keep up the good work."

"Thank you so much," Mr. Morton. "We'll continue to do our best and we'll let you know how he's doing."

Misty and Kerry were careful with the training of Charlie. Misty talked with Kerry often about Charlie's training schedule. "We have to be careful with him. He's still so young-just a two-year old and we want him to be strong and healthy for many years. He may be fast enough for the Kentucky Derby, but time will tell," said Misty.

"That's true. We certainly don't want him to get hurt," said Kerry. "I think he is talented. We'll just have to see how far his ability will take him. I don't think we should work him more than twice a week. That way he'll be eager to run, as well as healthy."

I wish I could run every day. After all, that's what I like and I want to be the best racehorse ever! I know that Kerry and Misty are protecting me, but this running stuff is cool. I can't wait to find out if I can beat some famous horses. Still, I'm so lucky that my trainers and their helpers take such good care of me.

Trouble at the Stakes Race

The day of the big Stakes race finally came. *It must be an important race today. Everyone seems excited about it and there are people and horses everywhere you look. Should I be nervous? Should I be scared? Will it seem different? We'll have to wait and see.*

Charlie was shining from head to toe. The weather was sunny and warm. He looked at the other horses who were galloping out to the starting gate. Most of them were ahead of him. He was shocked. He saw Buddy trotting along toward the gate. *Gee, he looks so muscular and grown up. I wonder how fast he'll run. I'll need to pay attention. I don't want to be distracted because my old friend is in the race.*

All the horses were standing nicely in the starting gate, waiting for the bell. The gates opened and the announcer yelled, "And they're off!" as all the horses left the gate. Buddy was leading and Charlie was just behind him, close to the rail. Charlie was relaxed, waiting for Joe to give him the signal to go to the lead. *I feel a little anxious. I don't want Buddy to get far ahead of me.* He felt Joe urging him forward with his legs. He flew to the front of the pack. He was eye to eye with Buddy. *I've got to try to win, even though Buddy is my friend. If I let him win, I wouldn't be doing my best.* Suddenly, Buddy was frightened by the noise of the crowd. He bolted to the side; bumping Charlie and making him lose his balance for a second. *I wonder why my left front foot feels sore. It's almost the end of the race so I think I can still win. I can't just give up, even if my foot hurts.* Charlie recovered just in time to cross the finish line first, but his front foot hurt. *I wonder what happened. I'm limping.* Joe noticed something was wrong and jumped off quickly. "What's wrong, Charlie? Let me look. Oh, I see. You've lost your shoe." He picked up Charlie's foot. "We'll have the blacksmith check it out." By now, Kerry and Misty had run to the racetrack to see what was wrong.

"He lost his shoe," Joe said. "I think he might have bruised his foot. He might have run a long way without his shoe. You might want to have the blacksmith check it out."

"Poor Charlie! You were so brave. "You still won, even though Buddy bolted to the side and banged into you. You showed you are a champion today. We'll take you right back to the barn and have Mr. Winston, the blacksmith take care of your foot," Misty said. She walked him to the barn and phoned Mr. Winston to come see Charlie right away.

"What do you think? Did Charlie bruise his hoof?" (his foot) Mr. Winston used some special tools to squeeze Charlie's hoof. When he reached one part, Charlie tried to pull his foot away so Mr. Winston knew that was the sore area. "Yes, I think he will be fine. We can put special padding under his racing shoes and he'll feel fine in a few days."

"Thank you so much," Misty said. "We'll give him a nice rest for a few days and see how he feels with the padded shoe."

Charlie relaxed and munched on his hay and oats in his stall for a few days. Then he was able to go out in the field to munch on the grass. *My foot is feeling almost as good as new now. I hope I can race again soon. I'm really lucky that Misty and Kerry don't make me run when my foot hurts. I could fall and really get hurt then.*

A week later, Kerry took Charlie out to the track for a little exercise.

Charlie was so happy he bounced up and down. "Ah, I see you're happy to be back here," Kerry said. "Let's see how you feel when you're running. She walked him into the starting gate. He heard the bell and sprang out of the gate. "That's it, Charlie. Just relax. You're doing fine," Kerry told him. "We'll just have a short work out today because we don't want to test your foot too much on the first time back." *It really feels good to be back. There's nothing like running. Winning is even more fun!*

Another Big Race

Kerry and Misty discussed the next step in Charlie's training. "He's responding well to training," said Misty. "He's paying attention to his work now and that's a big step forward. Where do you think he should race next?"

"I think we should try the Kentucky Stakes for two year olds. He'll be running against the best in the country then. We'll see how he does," said Misty. "After that, we'll let him mature more over the winter before we make plans for the big races in the spring," said Misty.

Racing Against the Best

"He's in tip top shape, Misty," said Kerry. "Just look at those muscles. He's grown a couple of inches recently. He's looking so handsome and grown up."

"That's the truth," said Misty. "He looks like he's well prepared for the race today."

Charlie was a mellow fellow, but he felt some unusual excitement in the air today. *I wonder how I'll do against the best horses.*

"Well, Charlie, we're together again," Joe said. "We'll find out how you measure up against some of the best two year olds around. My bet is you're going to surprise them all." *I felt Joe giving me a nice pat on the neck. He must have been telling me not to worry.*

Charlie listened for the bell. He shot out of the gate, ending up in second position. Joe kept him clear of any traffic jams. They stalked the leader, being careful not to let him get too far ahead. Charlie felt Joe moving his weight forward. "Okay, Charlie, show 'em what you've got," he said. Charlie raced along side of the leader. Now they were head and head. Charlie could see the other horse was tiring. He got a spurt of energy. He passed the leader. He was all alone crossing the finish line. The crowd cheered, "Go, Charlie, go!" Joe was stroking Charlie's neck. "Good job! I guess they all know you're one of the best now," Joe said. *I'm already thinking of my extra oats and my bubble bath. Life is good.*

Spring Training

"Charlie's doing great," said Misty. "He's strong and confident. He's much bigger than average. He must be at least 16.2 hands (the way you measure a horse) He's got a long relaxed stride and he knows when to really fly at the end of the race. That's his big finishing kick. I think we'll just put him in the Woodmont Stakes, as a prep for the Derby. He'll have three weeks to rest afterward. That should be plenty of time so he's not stressed."

Splashing Around in the Woodmont

It was Woodmont Stakes day. Crowds were everywhere. There was something different for Charlie, though. It had rained all night and the track was sloppy. He never ran in the mud before and he knew some horses didn't like it. *I wonder if it will be slippery racing in the mud. Maybe my shoe will fall off again. Maybe I'll just be stuck in it and my hooves won't move. It might be all right because I have my special rain shoes on. They're like rain tires, just made for the mud. They help keep me from slipping.*

On his way to the starting gate Charlie trotted, trying to get a feel for the mud. *It's not so bad. My rain shoes are giving me a good grip so I can concentrate on doing my best.*

Nine horses stood in the gate waiting for the bell. Charlie bounded from the gate, trying to get the best position. Mud splashed everywhere. Charlie was in fourth place, but not far from the leader. "Okay, Charlie, let's make our move," Joe said. Charlie was nearly pinned in by other horses. Joe moved him to the outside so Charlie had a clear run at the leaders. His long, sweeping strides took him past the first three horses. Now he was even with the leader. Joe said, "Come on, Charlie, you can do it. Just try you best. Give them the finishing kick," said Joe. Charlie put in the extra effort and surged ahead in the last few strides. *Whew! I wasn't sure which way that was going to go. Glad I tried my best and it worked out well. I had to make sure I believed I could win.* Jimmy came by to feed Charlie his vitamins and extra oats after he had his bubble bath. *I get lots of treats. I guess winning really pays off.*

Getting to Know Churchill Downs

Wow! That was a big test. I'm glad I can rest for a few days. I want to just play in the fields and chew on some daffodils. I think I ate all the tulips so they need a chance to grow back. Soon Charlie's vacation was over and it was time to go back to work to get ready for the Kentucky Derby. "Let's go to Church Hill Downs, Charlie. We're on our way to the Derby now. It's about the biggest race around, but you'll see some of the same horses you've seen before so there's nothing to worry about. Kerry will work you on the track so you get used to the way it feels," Misty said. Off they went to the Derby. *I've never seen so many barns. There are some horses working and others having their baths. It looks like a cool place. People are all dressed up too. The ladies are wearing some funny looking hats with flowers on them. Boy, I'd like to munch on them!*

The sun was just rising when Kerry galloped Charlie around the track.

Boy, I guess it gets so crowded here you have to get an early start. I'll work up an appetite for sure. However, I have to think about running right now. "It's only a few days till the Derby, Kerry," said Misty.

"Let's let him run a little. After that, he can cool off and relax," said Misty.

"Okay, I'll let him stretch out now," said Kerry. Charlie seemed to glide on the surface with amazing speed. Misty stood there wide-eyed, surprised at Charlie's speed. "That's enough, Kerry. Let us cool him off. He was fantastic. He's earned some extra oats today."

Derby Day

I feel great today. I can't wait to run. It's hard to believe this is really the day of the big race. Will I be the winner? I can't wait to find out.

Now we're on the way to the starting gate. Only a few minutes and we'll be off and running. I'm wearing number 3 today. Will that be my lucky number? The announcer said, "Ladies and gentlemen here is number 3, the favorite. He is Charlie the Horse. He's won every race but his first. The big question is can he win from the outside post number 11?"

That means I'll have farther to run. Good thing I had those extra vitamins. I might need them.

All eleven horses waited for the bell. Charlie stumbled at the start. *Wow! I almost fell. I have to try hard to catch up.* He was in seventh place when the horses got settled. "Don't worry, Charlie. We'll have to stay out of traffic, but we've got time to catch them," said Joe.

I might be in trouble, but I'll try to relax. It's no time to panic. Joe managed to get Charlie a good spot on the rail. Now they had climbed up to third place. "Okay, Charlie, let's go!" Charlie galloped even faster. One by one, he passed them. His old friend Buddy was the only one ahead of him. "Well, Buddy, I hate to do this, but I want to win so catch me if you can," Charlie said. He left Buddy in the dust and galloped past the finish line. *I did it! I won just about the biggest race around. I can't wait to tell the General.*

Misty and Kerry met him in the Winner's Circle. "Charlie, we're so proud of you," Kerry said. "You were great! Look how handsome you are wearing the blanket of roses that the winner of the Kentucky Derby wears! We're going to give you more than extra oats today. We're going to take you to Racing Haven so you can see your mom and your friends. I'll bet Mr. Bains will plan a special celebration for you." *It doesn't get better than that. Extra oats, a nice bath, AND a surprise trip to Racing Haven. Now I know what happens* when you work hard and think about your goals. Even though I'm the champion, I have to keep working hard so I'll be my best. I never want to be over confident and think no one will beat me. I know that even champions have days when they don't win. I can hardly wait to see my mom and I heard she has a brand new baby sister for me to meet. I can tell her about racing. Maybe she'll look up to me like I do to the General. I'll try not to only be the best racehorse I can be, but the best big brother, too.

Charlie wins the Kentucky Derby